I0726935

A Lineage of Waugh's

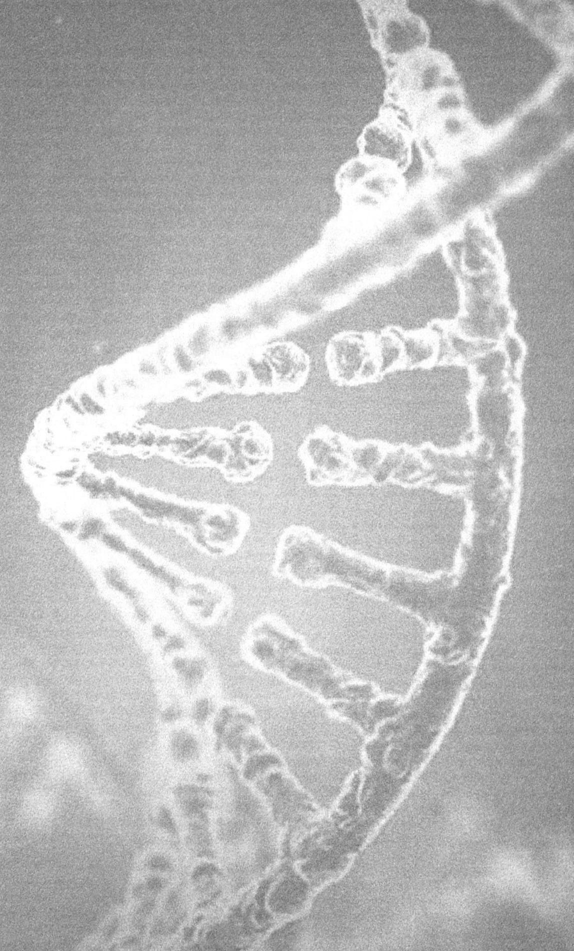

By: Russell Sullivan

Copyright @2021 by Russell Sullivan

All rights reserved. No part of this book may be reproduced in any form or by any electronic or mechanical means, including information storage and retrieval systems, without permission in writing from the publisher, except by reviewers, who may quote brief passages in a review.

This publication contains the opinions and ideas of its author. It is intended to provide helpful and informative material on the subjects addressed in the publication. The author and publisher specifically disclaim all responsibility for any liability, loss or risk, personal or otherwise, which is incurred as a consequence, directly or indirectly, of the use and application of any of the contents of this book.

WORKBOOK PRESS LLC
187 E Warm Springs Rd,

Suite B285, Las Vegas, NV 89119, USA

Website: https://workbookpress.com/
Hotline: 1-888-818-4856
Email: admin@workbookpress.com

Ordering Information:

Quantity sales. Special discounts are available on quantity purchases by corporations, associations, and others.
For details, contact the publisher at the address above.

Library of Congress Control Number:

ISBN-13:   978-1-956876-81-9 (Paperback Version)

                978-1-956876-82-6 (Digital Version)

REV. DATE: 09/12/2021

A Lineage of Waugh's

Also by Russell Sullivan

Two titles have been sent to Professional Publishers to mix with the greater world and perhaps one day allow for the migration of other unedited works. These are:

Going It Alone   published 2014

The Book Of Things   published 2016

Acknowledgments

To the double enténdre.

Prologue

World War I commenced after an arms race with a simple assassination as the trigger.

World War II is marked at Gdansk in Poland with the name of the German Ship that fired a fatal salvo.

The arms race will continue. This war will be different. Money a key motive, power another. It has been building in many countries. Today it began.

The arms race and motives will not abate. Tensions will run high. Revenge

Retribution

The hallmarks of this war.

Let this page mark its commencement.

1.

Have you ever asked the question why some traditions continue and others not? There is a question of much import to some, yet not to others, the latter forming the minority.

It is a question of lineage, peerage or ancestry.

This question enables dominion over nations, transference of wealth and influence and even just simple understanding for the multitude of whom am I? And where do I belong?

Throughout history the question of ancestry has provoked these and many other issues. Our thoughts turn though to another matter.

What is this?

Literature is artifice. To ancestry artifice is anathema, a conjurer's lie as artifice causes the fracturing of those many important issues of lineage discussed previously.

Simile.

Metaphor.

Tools; the tools of the writer. And artifice is a tool of the writer.

A master at his or her trade proudly displays their talents. Other wishing to emulate their feats can aspire to such heights of skill and in some cases only admire.

Evelyn Waugh was a literary Titan to some. Those who thumbed the pages of his writings revelling in literary artifice and all of literatures many other devices.

So why then did The Waugh tradition discontinue?

Where did lineage and the desire of those in later years to revel in works of this family disappear to?

It is something lamentable.

Something lost.

Tradition should continue, yet fatefully it did not. Those of us who have read and marvelled at the delights of Evelyn Waugh ruing the artifice of history.

A lost note scrawled in an alleyway has prompted an investigation into war? Its' lineages and histories. Unlike Evelyn Waugh the history of war itself is not subject to the rules of lineage, but artifice lends its hand to human behaviour and war, unlike our literary heroes knows no rules.

War has its own lineage, and like a mythical creature forms and reforms in many guises. History has altered the geographical landscape to an extent that the world of today makes a mockery of the historical world.

Easter Island the most remote location on Earth stranded in the midst of Oceanic vastness whose original inhabitants left naught but their statues themselves being banished from their island home.

Christmas Island is adjacent to the most sparsely populated continent with the exception of Antarctica where only those loveable penguins flourish. The inhabitants of these Island explorers on their way to a new life and a new world, trapped by political and social tragedy.

What then of Armageddon?

That destined and final War. If geography has so transpired to alter the socio-geographic landscape then the final battle, man's test after which lineage should be banished. There it could only be assumed be no battle after 'The Final Battle'.

War's lineage and the papery lineage that ordained this fate for humanity it can only be assumed will reach its culmination.

The bloodlines of The Arab titillate the equine historian and breeder. A horse breed renowned for its stature and coveted the world over. Wars bloodlines are those of humanity and although not coveted the world over, the stories of heroism and sacrifice make war as illustrious a bloodline as the equine Arab.

War thrives and will thrive on these images that for those who have been untouched or untainted by it can only be misconstrued. So will that Last Battle be The Last Battle, it is doubtful and wars lineage like The Arab will be admired and coveted by a zealous public. Our vagrant though is a different breed. Possibly he was touched by war forging that obtuse observation regarding one mysterious vehicle. Could this have been fancy and this delinquent a delirious relic that was part of society's detritus?

The bloodlines of the vagrant, unlike those nobler like the illustrious Arab, do not affect social desires or social outcomes like The Waugh family. This vagrant though had left a legacy; the question was what this scrawled notation meant?

2.

The year 2012 was the first clue in this mystery. This of course being the year in which the particular piece of detritus that was our scrawled message was located.

Twenty twelve or 2012 is of course an auspicious year for those with an offbeat mathematical sense of curiosity. Auspicious it marks the return of the "Twe's".

The Twe's are of course the odd coupling of the pronunciation of the two terms that comprise a single year. First appearing in the lexicon and calendar in the year Twelve Twelve (1212) and Twe's made only a brief appearance for that year before disappearing from language again.

Then in the year Twelve Twenty, after only a nine-year hiatus the Twe's resurfaced. There was jubilation amongst some as it was thought that perhaps the Twe's would not be seen again. Plague, pestilence, war and of course the all-important portent spelling impending doom from humanity that doom sayers have espoused over the years and millennia had been survived.

Now after a longer hiatus the Twe's had resurfaced. Cause for more jubilation as the elapsed period of eight hundred and ninety years was proof of the longevity of humanity. They had beaten the odds of those ill portents and the doom-sayers, plague was captive in bottles only allowed to show its head when the occasional viral infection or military chemical warfare laboratory dared tamper with the survival of humanity.

The Twe's were cause for celebration. And the Twenty First Century knew how to celebrate. Libation, licentiousness, libido and liberty the hallmarks of this new age.

1212 was not that near thousand years ago. Humanity had exceeded the celestial clock in its development and rather than maturing from a toddling three year old as it was considered those who lived in the twelfth century were by a somewhat conceited twenty first century man to a six year old; this maturity model based upon a 'social' model more akin to geological ageing than the ageing of persons.

Man, and woman, equal (or seen by some as such) in this twenty first century were almost middle aged. Mature beyond this notional social maturity models six years and heading towards the status of that wise elder.

The Twe's of course would recur in another eight years' time as they did in the first cycle in the year Twenty Twenty (2020). For another nine years people could embrace this recurrence. Then the Twe's would disappear until the year Twenty One Twelve. Recurring so frequently in this the bounteous century of the Twe.

Until of course the clock ticks over and the Third Millennia is reached. Twe' less and barren. Humanity will be bereft of the Twe's for many a year. The question some may ask is if that wise elderly maturity status is so near, what will the modern human social maturity is when the Twe's next appear after the Third Millennia.

What does this matter? It is important to understand that mysteries such as our scribbled note do not simply render themselves apparent. Thinking is required and in a manner akin to the Twe reasoning process this person will seek out the answer to that unusual notation.

So that we may continue on our course of discovery one particular lineage shall be 'put to bed' figuratively speaking. An unusual pair of Twe's was coincidentally referred to within the first pages of this book.

The first twelve marking the month of origin of the name that was later associated with Christmas Island; December. The second twelve of the pair being the sum of a group known as The Apostles who are associated with events in a Post-Christmas world. Easter Island figuratively marks the beginning for the second twelve when they were left without the guidance of their Christmas benefactor to provide guidance on their own.

These Twe's, unlike our recurring calendar based sequence considered unlikely to have recurred as there are no records as such or to recur.

One lineage then has marked its passage across time through markings and naming upon Earth's many places. Our other lineages of Twe's are marked by the passage of time itself. And our vagrant has left a clue. That clue being based in time itself as are these notations of the Twe's.

3.

Local areas of urban communities are usually administered by some form of Government. This form of Government being administered by itself in many cases by a higher form of Government.

Within this hierarchy was the answer to the first riddle regarding our vagrant. For Government has an interesting characteristic. It is organised and it takes its designated role in the community very seriously.

One of these roles is Public Health. The rubbish or detritus that is spread across society has been the cause of some of those plagues that decimated human populations, from this calamity the subways and drains of London were formed as a basis for other cities to follow.

London was, like Rome of old, the modern city of administration. It was science and industry rather than legions forging a social structure that was exported not unlike the products of the Industrial Revolution. Time once again stayed its hand and like Twe's enabled this administrative cycle to replenish itself regularly. So it was that the city of Melbourne, Australia hosted the twenty twelve detritus campaign.

At a point far South of Christmas Island on its northern borders Melbourne had like many cities its share of vagrants. Those without homes or the means to obtain them. A sole ship from England whose administrative inclinations had been in part transported to the continent of Australia had founded this continent as part of Europe.

Many years later a single round the world sailor had landed upon his home shores and commenced a 'Clean Up Australia' campaign. This annual event finding its roots in the detritus that this person had witnessed upon the high seas.

Administration is like the Twe's. Regular and recurring and interestingly like those Twe's subject to fluctuation in these cycles. Rubbish, as stated by those who many years prior in Europe who had suffered from the effects of plague, needs regular removal.

Public health met with public approval and administrative wheels of Government were applied most assiduously to this task. And our vagrant had left their note within the confines of a rubbish can within this city of Melbourne.

Those familiar with the character James Bond, famous as the suave espionage expert or spy in both book and film would understand what lead a foot weary traveller down that alleyway to find this strange note.

The sign on the wall read:

For those Bond lovers

Do you remember Pussy Galore?

Feast your eyes

This sounds possibly tawdry however my intention was not to visually gobble a gallery of pussies as those who are familiar with the slang derivation may think. It was simple curiosity.

Pussy Galore as it turned out was a pet shop. The owners took a somewhat licentious avenue to marketing. On the way down that rather unillustrious alley the reason for the name became apparent. Graffiti has its place, many people may wonder where precisely that is most appropriate; however the walls of this alley were famous for their graffiti and as a result attracted quite a number of visitors.

The description of the graffiti, like the bond title is best perhaps left to the imagination. Was it this that drew the vagrant down this alleyway? Possibly one would think. It was certainly what had lured me with its jovial play on words. The result being my treasure, not bonds treasure but my note.

My mystery and it was this mystery that required resolution. It was time to make more formal enquiries.

4.

Our bloodlines are those not of war. War of course remembers those who have formed its bloodlines. Plaques and memorials register the tragedy while clubs and associations bond those who remained to remember them.

Our vagrant perhaps belongs to a different form of tragedy. Not Shakespearean in its scope or scale but minuscule and human. The tragedy for some and that some are unknown in their numbers is that society does not necessarily care to register or remember them.

These were the bloodlines that needed to be chased. For example, HXB an unusual vehicle labelled with Beretta we will identify during this tale and the trails of the vagrant who attempted to identify it and indeed its operator To whom, or what bloodline did they belong? Who if anyone would remember them?

Unfamiliarity has a most particular difficulty. As a woman labours through childbirth a person attempting to undertake a task with which they are unfamiliar will struggle. And as childbirth differs so can the effects of unfamiliarity strain different people in different ways.

Chance had provided me a mystery. Chance had also thrust me into unfamiliar territory. The pregnancy now over pangs of labour were starting to startle my subconscious.

Many an explorer must have thought, my subconscious deduced, that the way through unfamiliar territory was first to locate it. Knowing from my scrawled page the territory to be explored then with the explorative attitude in mind it was time to find a compass and set sail.

A short walk from that detritus filled alley was a suburban street. One could perhaps describe it as being, not ordinary as that can be construed as demeaning, but normal. In the middle of this street sat house number twenty seven, whose single brick façade and well-kept gardens hinted to the explorative mind that it may be worth visiting.

Knocking upon the front door after checking for the presence of any malicious hounds it was a pinch nosed, middle aged lady with wire framed spectacles who answered.

"Yes?" was her enquiring question.

"Hello Madame, excuse my interruption however I am in the midst of writing a book about this area and was wondering if you could answer some questions for me."

She appraised me suspiciously, and not inviting me into the abode provided the answer that little information would be forthcoming. "What would you like to know?"

Thinking quickly, this was after all an unfamiliar experience my response was "where would one best go to find information here for such a book?"

"Do you see that building behind you" she replied pointing to a small wooden church sitting in the middle of a parkland. "Those of us who are part of the parish go to the Why Not. Do you know of the Why Not?"

"No" was my response.

"Good, you are honest. During the height of the struggles in Northern Ireland those of us Anglicans, and that is an Anglican Church, had some concerns. You knew there was even Royal blood spilled in those years, Mountbatten.

Terrible, Terrible.

After that security was considered and some of us decided to visit The Lambs Head. That is a tavern nearby. Talking to the proprietor conspiratorially we requested that on Friday evenings an area be reserved for us.

The proprietor sensing a business proposition obliged. So we moved from the church to The Lambs Head out of public view. Our joke being that when people were asked to visit The Lambs Head they would gladly reply "Why Not." So we call it The Why Not and our Parish is Why Not.

Should you like information then visit The Lambs Head and provide them with this knowledge. On each Friday evening those of us in The Why Nots are by agreement given thirty minutes where we choose the entertainment for our patronage.

However, to glean more information you will need to be able to provide the proprietor with more knowledge than this. As time progressed our business ties grew and now the list of proprietors' names

is noted with those who were known to us.

There are three questions to be accepted at the Why Not?

There are:

Where is Why Not?

Name our first friendly proprietor at The Lambs Head?

How many weddings have been conducted there?

Answer these correctly and you will find out information more

readily.

Good day."

Having said that she closed the door leaving me standing upon the

step with the gnawing of stomach cramp. Growing labour pain,

where would this birth lead next.

5.

It was termed 'The Beirut Effect'. City after city around the globe succumbing to the dread civil conflict that embroiled what had once been described as 'a jewel'. That city denuded like a statuesque maiden and displayed grotesquely before the rest of this planet.

The Green Line that had divided Beirut had conspired to divide the world. This, a form of cruel joke on humanity that mocked it as they themselves derisively mocked with those Darwin Awards. Science mocking itself and humanity doing likewise.

The Green Line did not cut a swathe through the globe like the equator or those tropics of Cancer and Capricorn. It meandered like the Nile, languidly making its way throughout the planet and dividing those who sat astride its different banks.

Was it a Beirut type syndrome that would afflict Melbourne? Did HXB provide a portent of a division that had already spread its evil wings around the globe?

The automobile is a beautifully constructed explosive device. It is thought the exclamation of the first person to successfully detonate a vehicle exclaimed "nailed it." Petroleum with its fuel is a potent mixture and the gases it emits while not as easily ignited as in those cliff top disasters in the movies is still incendiary.

Liquefied Petroleum Gas under pressure, and items under pressure are usually more inflammable than those not under pressure, is made for detonation. Modern vehicles actually forming a death-trap for those unaware or not so cautious. Yellow and orange shirts mark those trained and so those who are unaware of the dangers know that where an orange or yellow shirt is visible that explosives and detonations can be undertaken with safety.

Was this the Hilux?

The fate of that vehicle and its inhabitants. An incendiary device that those yellow or orange shirts would be all too willing to illustrate. Only time would tell.

6.

Rumour has it, as rumour does that there was a Prelude to the war that was foretold in that City Of Melbourne. Another war, not an actual phoney war as described before but a phoney war that was a phoney war.

In the hills to the North of Melbourne lay the City Of Wangaratta. Three years prior to the forecast hostilities in Melbourne rumour told of a war. The assailants unknown however night time crescendos of heavy bombing and the tell-tale aerial trails of jet fighters told a story of their own.

You could imagine being a person sitting outside a remote farm, barbecue burning its warm evening coals, a fire lit to clean away autumns litter and a few cold ales to wash this down. A cat mewed nearby wanting to be stroked and the stars were all that lit the sky. The noise breaks this type of silence one can imagine like the peel of a Church bell on a dewy Sunday morning. Thud. Woomf. In the distance far from those in this maelstrom music plays in a surreal contrast to the bedlam being unleashed and savagery witnessed.

A person can only imagine, and one would say most likely never with the correct degree of affect as those who were caught within such carnage what it was like. Farm animals bolting, vehicles torn to shreds and, persons rendered to pulp.

It was though only rumour, and so that phoney war perhaps could best have been named for these events. Melbourne though, well what was it about this foretelling? It was time to investigate further.

Having ascertained that the response to a simple postulate "Why Not?" could provide untold riches in the form of information it was time to consider my next actions.

Of course The Lambs Head and a relaxing ale with the stereotypical buxom wench nagged at the mind's eye most alluringly. A problem though presented itself and Madame's brassiere was thrust from the mind as quickly as it had so tantalisingly made its entry.

Time and time stamps are a tradition dating back for many centuries. The postal service marking deliveries for persons a classic example of where the time stamp had left its own indelible mark on the world.

It was a time stamp that I considered necessary to obtain prior to plunging my thoughts into the buxom and vexatious issue of "Why Not?"

Time marks events in the same manner as time marks that postal item. Greenwich one day decreed by humanity as a geographical landmark from which time would be measured making this all the more accurate. However the rudimentary date and time method prior to complex geophysical mapping still sufficed in most instances.

The Council Borough, that for the purposes of consistency in nomenclature in these pages, shall be referred to as Why Not opened at 9 in the morning.

As I strode through the door to the counter surveying this scene the necessary directions were provided. The sign pointing to the right reading "Sanitation Services."

Thinking quickly and somewhat foolishly that "Sanitation Services" would be most appropriate I grinned and thought "Why Not?" proceeding in that direction.

A middle aged gentlemen greeted me at the counter almost suspiciously as my eyes thrust themselves in a strange lecherous way toward his abdominal region. "May I help you?"

Looking up quickly and correcting my thoughts I replied "Sorry, yes please. Could you tell me how often the garbage collection is made from the large trash containers near Pussy Galores'?"

The man looked back at me with a soft glare considering the meaning of Pussy Galore and looked as though he would, out of nothing but vengeful malice for my leering entry and the subsequent connection and connotation of Pussy Galore, not provide me with a response.

Making a coughing noise as if clearing his throat a deep voice stated "every two weeks." The voice stopped and a decisive look that read now please leave told me that this was all the information I would be provided with.

Departing the Council Burrough of Why Not there was a contented smile upon my visage. The information to establish with a degree of certainty the time stamping of my mystery note was now available.

Walking past a Postal Office it was time to visit The Lambs Head.

7.

There is a question regarding names. Our famous vagrant, famous to me due to the affect they had in instigating this inquiry, must have had a name.

While the notations that were recorded could be readily investigated the identity of many people is much more difficult to ascertain. This particular individual, being a vagrant, would be far more difficult to identify.

How then would such a search be undertaken? There are of course many cases where the identity of persons has required tracing. An example the simple question, who was the first Christian?

War of course lies uncomfortably with mutiny. The military and indeed nations require that persons follow the chain of command to borrow a military expression.

The reasons for this are many, and indeed the instances of mutiny are many. The Mutiny On The Bounty is recorded and enjoyed as an historical event as it played out with bold characters on the high seas and the ousted Captain made an intrepid sea voyage to safety.

That Captain was later made Governor of a small colony in the days of imperialism. Survivors of the mutiny being found on an idyllic Island, after having escaped the treachery of the ships to Paradise were hanged.

The prime mutineer as the story could be told was a Mister Fletcher Christian. Religion of course and holy wars enjoy a more than adequate historical lineage. Religious lineage like wars lineage begs the question. Who was the first Christian? The Church during the halcyon days of the crusades was of course not predominant but dominant as the secular force. From within histories pages a division emerged, a silent mutiny if you will.
Outside the scope of The Church and its ways Christianity evolved. Christians and Christian organisations neither predominant nor dominant yet occupying a secular stronghold of their own. Who started this rebellion? Who was in mutineer terms the first Christian?

People of course will spend days, months or even years poring over historical records to find such an answer. It was hoped that my search for the title of the elusive vagrant would not require such effort however like the name of that Christian it would be no easy task to complete.

This would be no different

Have you ever stood naked in the middle of a busy street at two o'clock in the afternoon?

This is how it felt doing all of this investigative type digging. It makes you think of the police doing their duty, there they stand but in fact are totally exposed. Traffic whizzes by as they point their fingers with starched white gloves.

It is possible that upon return to a station the conversation would be "how was duty Officer Briggs?" The reply nothing but a curt nod until Officer Adams walks in. "Told him he had erectile dysfunction, there I was totally exposed and he thought nothing of it. Just pointed at the traffic and said "keep moving.""

Walking into The Lambs Head was like this. You felt totally exposed, an outsider. The sign above the door read "Mark ye path for Hades beckons."

Eyes turned toward the interloper and the remains of a fire signalled the gateway to Hades. Cerberus slept on a rug fitfully nearby snoring as only a Great Dane can. How does a person break that ice, ask those probing questions in such an atmosphere?

certain event. People with mental illnesses have meltdowns. The brain and associated identity suddenly becoming disengaged with reality.

Societies as well have meltdowns. Was it possible that a pressure cooker was developing and that what was predicted was not as much a war, but a meltdown. Would a warm weather summery Melbourne become a Syria outcast by the Christian League due to icy relations between its residents.

Was there some sleeping illness, a festering sore that would engulf the city?

There is a group of people that society counts amongst its most unfortunate. The relationship between them and society having a duel impact that is considered more concerning than many another.

These are called missing persons.

Society counts them as lost, and those who search in vain for them are considered as unfortunate as those that are lost. Why people go missing is as varied a mystery as their disappearance itself.

Runaways.

People smugglers.

Mental disorders.

Death.

Just some of the many possible reasons that this list, growing year by year, haunts the world in which we live. Those who have lost these people do not have the ability to grieve correctly. Memorials and markers plus those signs pasted to posts with the face painted on and a plaintiff plea.

All illustrating a yearning.

The yearning to know.

It is interesting, that Why Not should have its origins in religion. The bastion of knowledge and security in matters relating to the passing on of persons.

Those who belong to the bastions of Why Not fortified by their knowledge while others, for reasons as mysterious as those missing persons have an uncertain yearning.

Why and how such a social dichotomy developed and remains is a mystery again. Should a person bother to consider such weighty matters as this, some would say Why Not and others Why.

The world is as mysterious as this mystery itself.

A police station exhibits lists of those considered missing, the doors or an interior poster fixed with just some of those faces. And it is those police who represent the face of societies missing persons and the hunt for that elusive answer as to their demise.

Time may pass, and memorials remain but until the answer to what became of missing persons is known there can be no rest for some. So to the police station it was.

Could that person, that one who wrote that note be one of those who for reasons of mental health or perhaps they were a runaway have inhabited the dark alleys?

Asking questions of the police regarding matters pertaining to missing persons is something like asking an actor what they consider of television or film.

Somehow it seems contradictory or incorrect. Yet the question needed to be asked of the police. So to the police station a visit was made and the question asked "do you know anything about the disappearance of persons in this area, and particularly one who may have spent time near Pussy Galores?"

A frosty glare was the response when asked for my credentials and telling them that I was no more than a passer-by interested in an unusual article that I had found.

The police not considering it worth the time dealing with a request of such a flippant nature regarding matters of such importance.

So, leaving the police station and all those questions about missing persons it was back to the real world. Society would always, until satisfactory answers were provided, as society always had asked those questions of those such as the police.

Can you tell me what happened to these people?

For myself, the quest for the meaning of my mysterious notation would need to follow a different path. And it was beginning to become apparent, that like those unfortunate missing persons no answer would be found.

9.

It was on the Pakistan Afghanistan border that the incident occurred. The term is friendly fire, or perhaps collateral damage, whatever idiomatic expression those military types coin for their mistakes.

Of course mistakes are understandable in conflict where mayhem possibly replaces order. Of interest to some was that after the event the analysis showed that those on the grounds had received some incorrect information.

The Pakistan Government and relations in the already strained region boiled over and supply lines were cut. What was not noticed was a strange dolphin etched on stones nearby.

Of course those in the affected area would think nothing of it, after all these are mysterious lands. In years to come perhaps they will ask what that dolphin was doing there. For now though the issue was not raised and the war raged on.

Her name was Vapid, or so she informed me.

I found her sitting on a wooden park bench beneath an Autumnal maple tree that glowed fiery reds and oranges. Dressed in heavy but marked garb she had heavy-lidded eyes that spoke of stupor.

Expecting this it was a surprise to find the spritely young lass to be much more erudite than her name implied. Impressions of course can be misleading and upon questioning as to the origins of her name she simply said that it was her nom de plume.

Then turning to me she asked quite frankly was I expecting intercourse? Taken aback the answer was a stricken "no." Was that a look to say do you think me not worth it that suddenly flashed past those eyes.

I was being tested. Checked over to see whether my acquaintance was worth anything. Odd to be considered in such a manner by a person some in the social strata would consider an inferior.

And it is perhaps this notion and social strata that constructed and enabled the notion of inferiority that caused so much distrust and consternation. My task was to get beyond this, and not have another situation like The Lambs Head.
Would intercourse achieve anything? I asked. "Only to starch your ball-bearings" she replied.

"Then why ask?"

"To see if that was what you were after, usually that's the case."

"Let me assure you it is not" was my reply "I am trying to solve a riddle. And it concerns a person in this area with whom and which I am not acquainted."

She nodded and asked if I was from the police.

"No. Just somebody who found an intriguing item and decided to follow it up." my reply.

"Suppose you're one of those Bermuda Triangle types. Know anything about it?" those eyes suddenly lifted and asked as an appraising question.

"Not something that particularly interested me as a subject of inquiry" my response.

"Then why bother with its puzzle. If the Enola Gay and those types of things aren't of interest then who cares about what happens here."

The lady certainly made habit of checking out her visitors, starched ball-bearings or not. Still progress was being made.

"Was it not The Mary Celeste?" my reply

She smiled as if to say caught you and asked how I knew about The Mary Celeste and not The Bermuda Triangle.

This was seeming to go nowhere so in desperation I offered a meal, or hot beverage. The smile broke even further and she pointed to a nearby café and requested a large hot chocolate and some cake.

We adjourned and seated ourselves at a table. Red and white check vests spoke of a pizza establishment but the menu was quite varied. Ordering drinks and beverages Vapid looked at me and asked what I wanted to know.

Telling her the story of the note and producing it the question was did she know of any person who was known in the area and could be found such as herself in Pussy Galores alley.

Pussy Galore, don't tell me you weren't after intercourse. What were you doing there?

"Wondering what it was all about."

"Rubbish, you wanted strippers. None there go to the other end of this street and about three blocks to the left you'll find what you're after. And don't come back looking for intercourse again after."

Assuring her that strippers and intercourse were not my intention it was time to turn the tables I decided. Asking slightly more assertively where Vapid came from she raised her eyebrows again.

"It's what they called me since school. Lived here for most of my life and so people all know me as Vapid. It is something that you get stuck with."

"What about family?"

"Passed away, no jobs not when they think you're Vapid so it was just a matter of surviving. Do it and sometimes even have intercourse, but only sometimes. Have to be careful."

The conversation was turning out not to be quite as expected. The lady was more than appealing beneath those heavy robes. Hair with a purple tinge cut short, a round pretty face and figure that carried a few extra pounds taking it from titillating to tantalising.

The question entered my mind, what should someone do?

As though reading my mind she said not to give her a sympathy vote, and not to entertain any thoughts beyond cake and hot chocolate. Standing as if to leave she stated that nobody frequented Pussy Galores alley that she was aware of and departed back to the park bench.

Nodding at her as she strode away my thoughts turned to the question where to next?

That answer was as difficult as the question of who was responsible for my mystery note.

10.

Tragedy and travesty are both manifestations of language that is used to conjure melancholy, and imbue enthusiasm. Cause loves effect and causes love pathos.

The tyrant, demagogue and many other persons and states have required cause to affect their rule. What is a tyrant and is this simply subjective? After all a ruler may simply be termed thus for no greater reason than envy or desire on the part of an interloper or usurper.

This set of circumstances had conspired in the years before the Twe's had re-emerged in Libya. Ruled by, subjectively a tyrant, a phenomenon that like those Twe's had thrust itself onto the world stage had conjured all of pathos's energy as The Arab Spring unfolded.

Would, like the Twe's The Arab Spring have a recurrent cycle? This would be cause for concern perhaps, unless tragedy and travesty and the resultant melancholy are somehow deemed healthy for society overall.

Lineage needs not always one would think be best followed. And in the year of the Twe's a country euphoric after the results of the previous year stood on uneasy feet trying to purge that tyrannical past but perilously armed for a future of dissent.

Transition is the enemy of lineage, altering its course in a way that precludes revival or resurgence. Transition though has its perils and while Lenin and Russia may have found their way to The Union Of Soviet Socialist Republics even this behemoth had surrendered relatively meekly to Glasnost.

What then of this mysterious area locally known as Why Not?

Attached to a wall were a series of posters. One way to unlock the secrets of any area is by those bills pasted to the walls of telegraph poles and buildings.

The uppermost bill was an invitation to a concert.

"Music has moved on, do you recall the days of Beethoven and Mozart. Those BIG symphonies. Come and enjoy the BIG symphony sound with our chamber quartet."

Below this was a poster that read:
"WANTED: DEAD OR ALIVE

MY FINANCE ADVISOR.

THE ORCHESTRA MAY HAVE DOWNSIZED THEIR INSTRUMENTS WHY DID THEY HAVE TO GO THE SYMPHONIC ROUTE."

A further notation read:

WANTED: CONDUCTOR WHO IS NOT TONE DEAF.

It seemed that this quiet little corner of the world had, like many others its disparate groupings and opinions. From the musical aficionados to a very Marxist sounding underbelly.

On an adjacent post was another colourful placard that caught my eye. Large script letters and a gaudy picture of a woman, with the male jockstrap showing from beneath a raised skirt.

Included on the poster was another picture wearing boxing gloves drawn as a caricature of a short man in military uniform with a square trimmed moustache.
The placard reading:

HARRIET THE HERMAPHRODITE

VS HARRY THE HITLER

The bout, seemingly part of a travelling festival, to be seen that evening at nine o'clock.

It would seem that Why Not managed to attract a very eclectic and some may say eccentric entertainment. Was this due to the unusual nature of Why Not and its mysterious past?

Did those not from the area, like Area 51 and Roswell so famed amongst conspiracy theorists, know of Why Not and visit with such unusual displays to coax the Why from Why Not?

Walking further down the street and viewing the differing displays a further item caught my eye. A notice board for jobs wanted and jobs to be had included the local trading market section.

The For Sale items ranging from motorbikes, to televisions, dogs, cats and then one more item.

FOR SALE

TOYOTA HILUX

CALL REG ON 0476 433 790

Only those genuinely interested should bother.

Sudden excitement and adrenalin surged through my system. All my enquiries to date resulting in what could be summarised as a Vapid waste that in any form of discourse would most probably, given what was known, only lead to Why Not?

Of course Why Not is a meaningless statement in this context and that was exactly where my enquiries had lead. The Hilux though had surfaced.

Could this be the phantom vehicle?

Reg conjured an image, not entirely unlike Harriet The Hermaphrodite but with a workers singlet rather than the jockstrap, heavy beard, broad shoulders and bulging biceps.

A voice to match the lumberjack build the type of person to have christened their vehicle Beretta.

Christened.

That, like Harriet The Hermaphrodite was the way people treated their vehicles. The name, chosen to represent the character of the vehicle given it recently after purchase with a select group who represented the Godparents.

What would the Godparents of Beretta be like, and what type of christening ceremony would it have been.

One would think Reg and others, after acquiring such a beast, would have taken to the great outdoors. "Let's see what she can do in the rough stuff" the Godparents and other familial members requesting.

It was starting to make sense.

Should then a call be made to Reg?

Why Not.

11.

The Assad Government of Syria was caught between a rock and a hard place. International condemnation on the one hand and internal dissent on the other.

Governments cannot tolerate dissent, that is the one constant about Government. In Syria the city of Homs was recorded for the atrocities. They died in their tens, then their hundreds and finally their thousands. Brutality met by brutality and a war that had not seemed inevitable in this once more peaceable and stable Middle East province had become inevitable.

Of course those who had changed sides, especially military faced the risk of court martial and execution. Such is the tragic choice of the military and the even more tragic death trap that internal dissent had fomented. Those tanks not before seen moved down the streets and dissent was dealt a mortal blow.

Who would be victor? Death of course. Death always wins and those thousands showed just how mighty death can be. History will judge the Assad regime and those who decided to stand against it. Will there be those executions for those who dared to challenge the state or will the state topple.

And what would death have to say about all this?

Death walked around the corner, scythe in hand and asked if I knew anything about HIV.

Looking at this odd fellow my only response was a somewhat perplexed "pardon?"

There was, many a year ago an advertising campaign with the grim reaper trying to stop the spread of HIV. My job is to act as what the scientists are calling a cognitive recollective social artisan.

The role is multi-purpose.

Firstly to try and ensure the message of AIDS is still recalled within the wider community.

Secondly. To gather information, for the scientific community, on the effects and recognition of advertising and especially those such as the Grim Reaper within the general populace.

Thirdly. Place any items of rubbish that may be found littering the side-walks in appropriate receptacles as part of a public cleanliness campaign.

Nodding my head at death as if to say that this was completely understandable, the thought occurred to me regarding my article of rubbish.

"Do you frequent Pussy Galores?" I asked.

"Pardon. What would death be doing staring at the naked female genitalia in profundity?" death replied looking perplexed.

Now it was my turn to be perplexed.

My role, as part of a campaign to understand the location and displacement of items of litter, for the purposes of reporting to the literary community, is to dress as an idiot and see if this affects anybody.
As for why death would want to spend time gazing fixedly at a

profundity of female pubis, add that to a list of questions for the scientific community and cognitive recognition programs.

"Do you know where I could find some?" death asked.

"Find some what?" my response.

"Female pubis, a career as death makes it a bit hard for me to come by." Was his disconsolate reply.

Thinking of Vapid it was considered that maybe death and Vapid may actually hit it off. Silently congratulating myself I pointed death to the park that Vapid and I had our discussion in.

Death looked at me excitedly, which struck me as somewhat ironic really, and my parting remark was "get yourself a bike and see if you can entice her to look at your ball bearings."

Death just nodded looking at me in a strange way that only death could and walked in the direction of a local bike shop. Fascinated that death would so easily take instruction I gave the idea no further thought and decided to recommence my search.
The only issue was, where and how to do this?

It seemed that there was really no alternative but to give up the chase. That note grasped in my hand for a final read it was time to reconsider my options in life.

Hoping that death and Vapid would be happy together I strolled out of Why Not into a future that forever would be affected, like those with HIV by that grim reaper campaign, by a small slip of paper found in a notoriously named alley in an oversized trash can.

<h1 style="text-align:center">*12.*</h1>

Is there inevitability about war? The Twe's will pass and in this millennium of Twe resurface on a recurrent basis more prevalent than before.

A marker has already been placed in times eye for this second decade of that millennium. In 2014 the country of Afghanistan, marred by its own lineage of wars, has been designated for removal of forces from abroad embroiled in a conflict there.

Will then 2015 see the marking of a lineage other than war? Afghanistan in the majestic shadows of The Himalayas may perhaps find majesty within its people and its borders.

Evelyn Waugh represents an individual, albeit due to circumstance one considered different from those of us who would be described as comprising the masses.

Being one of the masses makes a person inconspicuous, histories non-entity. The masses destined to consider the likes of Evelyn

Waugh in a way that only the masses can. And what is this way?

This person, not being one of those masses could not make such a judgment. The masses although individual and inconspicuous make their own judgments and decisions. What then would the masses think of war and wars lineage? Will 2015 mark an era of positivity amongst the masses with the passing of one war heralding a new era?

War is not kind to the masses. They are often the victim, unable to fend off the machine that presses against them. To the masses then a tribute:

> ***Evelyn lay your head in restful sleep***
> ***Lines of words marking your ancestry***
> ***Those of us not of such an ilk***
> ***Would hope history takes a lesson***
> ***Us masses to remember it by***
> ***And to judge us by our own actions***

Evelyn Waugh passed on in the year 1966. And, as Afghanistan makes its plans one way or another, like all those others within these pages to determine its future it was time to do the same.

Having failed to ascertain, and ascertained that my investigative skills were such that the details of that mysterious note would remain just that, mysterious. It was necessary to conclude matters.

An interesting difficulty with the story is not the start or middle although they have their problems, it is in the ending. What is a story worth without a good ending?

Deciding that Vapid, and her unusual self, was such an invaluable contributor the story would be worth little without her aid. And something worth little, in the modern economy of the Twe's rather than earlier years, would colloquially be called a Buck.

That Buck translating from the slang to mean a dollar.

As Vapid and I sat and discussed the region whose nom de plume was Why Not, a middle aged male strolled past our seats. Vapid looked at him and then me, suddenly asking "do you know who that was?"

Thinking that for me to know then the person must be of some importance, or perhaps famous, I looked closely. Nondescript people are just that, nondescript. Which is why they were, rather appropriately, called nondescript.

This important or famous person was rather nondescript making it difficult to make an astute observation as to their identity. Turning back to Vapid my response was a very precise "no. Why do you ask?"

Vapid looked me in the eye, which when those eyes staring at you are somewhat heavy-lidded, can be somewhat disconcerting. Yet, stare she did to make her point. "Listen to what I am going to say."

"There is a story of a man, a man who whenever there is a problem, told the tale of how a problem shared is a problem solved.

Whenever there was a problem, people would go to this man to seek advice, and using his famous adage he would quickly hand them on to someone else for assistance.

Any problems concerning this man were also very quickly handed on to others for 'the benefit of the greater good, a collegiate communal approach' as he describes it.

Over time as more people came to see him the pattern became entrenched. A joke then became known, within the collegiate community.

"Where are you going?" people would ask.

"To see Buck." Would be there laughing response.

"Good luck with it then, see you when Buck sends you back." And they would laugh and go their way.

"That man is Buck."

I laughed, and looked back at those disconcertingly heavy-lidded eyes to say that I understood.

So that story ended, as shall this one, the details of that note handed on to those who read these pages. Passed on as one would, colloquially pass the Buck.

For those who sit at tables and chairs and laugh as Buck passes by, knowing who the Bucks are in the world, it is time for me to join the ranks of Bucks. What is this story worth, probably only that colloquial Buck? Such is its start, middle and end.

Yet, in the greater communal collegiate world the Buck has been passed to those who would try to solve that most unusual mystery of mine.

Sitting with a smile at having, albeit unsuccessfully, completed this tale my attention was drawn to a passing vehicle.

Heavy bodied with a tarpaulin covering the tray back. Word 4x4 marked on the rear side which was spattered with mud. The white frame marred by this uncleanliness and the rear window highlighted by a sign.

BERETTA

Staring in amazement as it passed, my thoughts wondered. Did this mean something?

And if so, what?

www.ingramcontent.com/pod-product-compliance
Lightning Source LLC
Chambersburg PA
CBHW040546170726
48295CB00012B/606